Dear Parents:

Congratulations! Your child is taking the first steps on an exciting journey. The destination? Independent reading!

STEP INTO READING® will help your child get there. The program offers five steps to reading success. Each step includes fun stories and colorful art or photographs. In addition to original fiction and books with favorite characters, there are Step into Reading Non-Fiction Readers, Phonics Readers and Boxed Sets, Sticker Readers, and Comic Readers—a complete literacy program with something to interest every child.

Learning to Read, Step by Step!

Ready to Read   Preschool–Kindergarten
• big type and easy words • rhyme and rhythm • picture clues
For children who know the alphabet and are eager to begin reading.

Reading with Help   Preschool–Grade 1
• basic vocabulary • short sentences • simple stories
For children who recognize familiar words and sound out new words with help.

Reading on Your Own   Grades 1–3
• engaging characters • easy-to-follow plots • popular topics
For children who are ready to read on their own.

Reading Paragraphs   Grades 2–3
• challenging vocabulary • short paragraphs • exciting stories
For newly independent readers who read simple sentences with confidence.

Ready for Chapters   Grades 2–4
• chapters • longer paragraphs • full-color art
For children who want to take the plunge into chapter books but still like colorful pictures.

STEP INTO READING® is designed to give every child a successful reading experience. The grade levels are only guides; children will progress through the steps at their own speed, developing confidence in their reading.

Remember, a lifetime love of reading starts with a single step!

P9-CQS-713

Visit us on the Web!
StepIntoReading.com
rhcbooks.com

Educators and librarians, for a variety of teaching tools, visit us at RHTeachersLibrarians.com

ISBN 978-1-5247-6862-1 (trade) — ISBN 978-1-5247-6863-8 (lib. bdg.)

Printed in the United States of America   10 9 8 7 6 5 4

nickelodeon

Sunny Day™

ROCK STARS!

adapted by Courtney Carbone

based on the teleplay "Band Together" by Rachel Vine

illustrated by Susan Hall

Random House 🏠 New York

Sunny runs a hair salon.
Her best friends are
Blair and Rox,
and her dog, Doodle.

They are in a band called
Sunny and the Sun Rays!
They will enter
a big talent show.

Sunny sees her friends
at the talent show.
Cindy is making
the tallest cake in town.

Junior has a magic act
featuring a special box.
Lacey and KC will juggle.

Lacey wants to outshine
Sunny and the Sun Rays.
She and KC hide
Doodle's drums.

The band notices that
Doodle's drums are gone.
They cannot perform
without drums!

Sunny has an idea!
She gets some
pots from Cindy.

Sunny always has
lots of salon supplies
with her.

She covers the pots
with shower caps.

Now Doodle needs
drumsticks.
Sunny gives him combs.
Perfect!

Lacey will have
to find another way
to stop Sunny's band.

Lacey and KC make a path of dog treats that leads to Junior's magic box.

Doodle follows the path
of treats.
Lacey locks him
in Junior's magic box!

Where is Doodle?
Sunny, Rox, and Blair
look everywhere.

Sunny finds Junior.
He has lost the key
to his box!

Junior is worried
about his trick.

It is time for Junior
to do his magic show.
Sunny helps him.

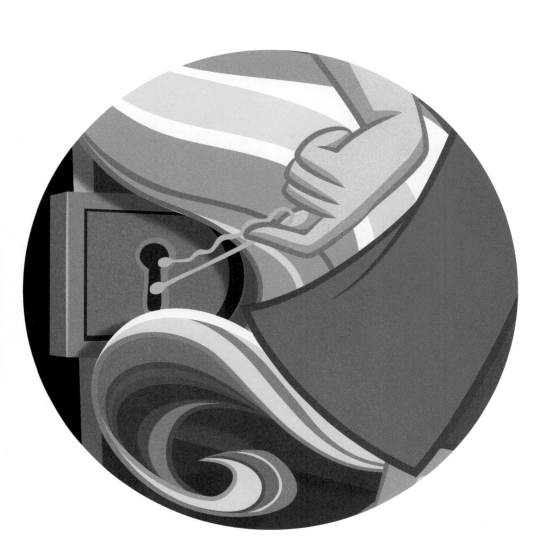

When no one is looking,
Sunny uses a bobby pin
to unlock the magic box.

Junior says
the magic words.
Doodle jumps out
of the box!

Doodle is back.

Sunny and the Sun Rays
rock out.

The crowd goes wild!

Keep smiling,
keep styling,
and keep rocking!